The Boy with the Narwhal Tooth

Greenland Missing Persons #1

featuring Constable Petra "Piitalaat" Jensen

Don't miss novella #2 in the
Greenland Missing Persons series
The Girl with the Raven Tongue

Introduction

There are two questions about my writing that scare me the most. The first is *how many books have you written?* I've never been good at mathematics, but it should be an easy answer, a straightforward sum – just add them all up. But I've been exploring Greenland through my stories for a little while now, through novels, novellas, short stories, and collections, even poems and essays. So much so, my stock answer is usually twenty novels and twenty-five novellas, but I'm not sure about that anymore.

The second question is equally frightening, perhaps even more so. *What order should I read your books in?* Or *which book should I start with?* I have prequels and sequels and stand-alones. Some of my books are set in the past; others are set far into the future. They are nearly all linked through one character or another. I write these stories as I think about them. There is no grand plan, but perhaps a few rules of thumb. But let's keep it simple, and start with the book you have in your hands or on your eReader, phone, or tablet.

The Boy with the Narwhal Tooth is set at the very beginning of Petra Jensen's career as a police constable in Greenland. It is by no means a typical career, nor are these stories to be confused with the real police work in Greenland. They are *inspired* by what I witnessed and experienced, and then injected with a heavy dose of myth, culture, tradition and drama. Regardless of the accuracy of the details, *The Boy with the Narwhal Tooth* is story #1 in Petra's police career.

I call her Petra, but if you've read any of my other stories, and if you've met Constable David Maratse, you'll know he calls her *Piitalaat*.

These are her stories.

Let's begin with this one.

Chris
June 2020
Denmark

The Boy with the Narwhal Tooth

Greenland Missing Persons #1

Part 1

It's a cliché, I know, but it really did start with a telephone, an empty desk and a generous new police commissioner, giving my career a gentle shove in the right direction. Fresh out of Greenland's Police Academy, my boots were still buffed, and my jacket had that factory smell of wax and freshly stitched seams. During training, I had become expert at flattening my hair, tugging it into a tight ponytail that I had learned to flick out of the way of opportunists' hands, when sparring in the gym. I had also learned to tone down my perfume and scented shampoos, allowing myself just enough scent to arouse interest from my single colleagues – *I graduated from a police academy, not a nunnery.* And, aside from my utility belt swagger – the *only* weight I wanted on my hips –I had learned that while a clean sidearm could be seen across a crowded room, a speck of dust or fluff in the trigger guard could be seen a mile away. In short, I was ready for duty, ready to be hazed, to give as good as I got, to respect experience, but also to make the most of my twenty-three years, and to put my orphan past behind me. I had, figuratively and physically, big boots to fill, measured by my own aspirations and a less than comfortable past.

Unfortunately, during my first weeks on the

job, I did little more than get in the way.

"Training is over, Jensen."

I must have heard that little gem about a thousand times in the first week, and a thousand more in the second. One man in particular made a point of working it into each and every situation imaginable, from pulling out of the parking lot, to making coffee. Sergeant Kiiu "George" Duneq was always there. I could never shake him. To be fair, he was partly responsible for making sure I learned the ropes, that I transitioned from newly graduated police constable, to a useful working part of what he seemed to think was a well-oiled machine. Sergeant Duneq was my supervisor, and I spent far too much time hating him when I should have been paying more attention to a briefing. He seemed to enjoy it when I stumbled, adding comments about my physical appearance – *too pretty for police work*. I was, I will admit, far prettier than him, but that was all I had on him. His girth, the way his utility belt had extra holes in it, belly hanging over the buckle, like his jowls melting over the collar of his dirty shirt – these things were the only things I could comment on, and only when I was alone, or sometimes with Constable Atii Napa, when we had a night off together.

"Fluff on his trigger guard," she said, shouting over the beat and thump of *Mattak*, Nuuk's most popular nightclub. "I saw it, I tell you."

"But no one else did, I bet you," I shouted back.

Even after a few drinks, blinking in the purple blue swathes of disco lights, I could still picture Sergeant Duneq's greasy black hair, and the tiny flakes of skin clinging to his bushy eyebrows. I flinched when Atii dropped her glass, looking at the door expecting to see him there, telling me with a fleshy grin that *training was over*.

He didn't have to tell *me* that, but Atii could have used a few reminders, I thought, as I slipped out of the booth and tugged her into my arms. When we graduated together, the new police commissioner addressed our class of six police graduates, reminding us to look out for each other. He told us we were never off duty, and if a colleague needed help, we were to give it, unquestioningly, but I would have done it anyway. So I helped Atii home that night, undressed her, wiped her sweaty brow, tucked her into her large double bed, and crawled in beside her. I turned her head to one side each time she rolled onto her belly, and then held her hair each time she crawled out of bed to pitch her drinks into the toilet.

I reminded myself that this was the life I had dreamed about, the career I had worked hard for. But now that my duty days and nights were spent with *Sergeant Jowls*, as I called him, and my nights off became a mix of controlled abandon and Atii's projectile vomiting, I did begin to wonder if it would ever change for the better.

Luckily for me, it did, the very next day.

Part 2

Commissioner Lars Andersen, new to Greenland and newly arrived from Denmark, had a secret. I wasn't sure how many of my colleagues had noticed, the commissioner seemed to prefer short communiqués, and even shorter email messages. Most of my younger colleagues, digital natives such as myself, probably didn't notice, but I imagined that a few of the older hands, especially the administrative staff, would soon query the commissioner's short form communication, if they hadn't already done so. Danish was my first language, and it was one of the few things I was really good at, with English and German a close second. Greenlandic, the language of my country, however, escaped me. But the Danish that the commissioner preferred was short to the point of simplistic. It wasn't that he didn't have a flair for language; he held vigorous speeches with plenty of adjectives and anecdotes. But I had seen a pattern in his communication, and when the opportunity presented itself, I asked him about it.

That opportunity came shortly after a long sigh and a string of quiet but enthusiastic curses. I was in the outer office of the administrative wing of Nuuk Police Station, ignoring the persistent beep of a *call waiting* tone from the telephone at an empty desk at the far end, furthest from the commissioner's office. Sergeant Jowls had told me to wait while he added the finishing touches, as he called them, to his supervisory report, something he enjoyed reminding me of whenever he felt I needed what he called a *confidence boost*. The number of reminders I received seemed to increase as I gained increasing competence – and confidence – in different skills, not least when we were out on patrol, and I was driving. I smiled at the recent image of Sergeant Jowls squeezing in behind the steering wheel to show me how to drive on icy roads, as if the first two hours of the patrol didn't count.

The commissioner cursed again, louder the second time, and I heard him toss a sheaf of papers onto his desk, before he stormed out of the office, fingers gripping a bright red coffee mug.

"Constable," he said, pulling up short at the door of his office. "How long have you been there?"

"A few minutes, Sir," I said. I focused on his coffee mug, wondering if it would crack under the pressure of the commissioner's frustration.

"Long enough, I suppose."

"Yes, Sir."

The commissioner was taller than most of the police officers in Nuuk, but a little shorter than Sergeant Gaba Alatak, the bold and bald leader of the police Special Response Unit, the SRU. Atii had her sights on him already, and, in a moment of weakness, I admitted that I understood why. I caught myself daydreaming and refocused, dialling in as the commissioner asked me a question.

"You don't speak Greenlandic, do you?"

"No, Sir."

"Any reason?"

I wondered just how much to say, and how much he might have read about my past. The commissioner turned his back on me to refresh his coffee, and I took a moment. Somehow I needed to condense my early years in the Nuuk Children's Home, the years of teasing through school, and the sudden light at the end of the tunnel that came with a single room in the gymnasium Halls of Residence. It was about the same time when I discovered a love for the order and rules of grammar and a certain mixer called *Mokaï*.

"I just never learned, Sir," I said, when he turned around. "There were other things to deal with."

"Okay," he said, cradling the mug in his hands as he leaned against the sideboard. "But you know Danish?"

"Yes," I said.

"Good grade at gymnasium?"

"Yes." I blushed, and then again when I realised Atii would tease me about it forever, just like she did in gymnasium.

"Constable," the commissioner said, with a nod to his office. "If you've got nothing better to do just now, perhaps you could help me with something?"

"Of course," I said, taking a step forward.

He paused at the door, frowning at the desk in the corner of the long outer office.

"That phone has been beeping all morning. And the staff," he said, gesturing at the empty desks, "are on a course. Back after lunch. All calls have been diverted to the front desk, but they must have forgotten that one. Never mind," he said, with a nod for me to walk ahead of him. "I'm sure someone will answer it later."

"Yes, Sir," I said, sitting down on the chair in front of his desk as he slumped onto the office chair behind it.

"There's a report due," he said, setting his coffee down beside a sheaf of untidy papers. "And I just can't get my head around it. Do you think you could have a look at my notes?"

"Yes, Sir," I said, wondering what Sergeant Jowls would think when he arrived.

Part 3

The commissioner's words were a mess. I said nothing for a full minute. He sipped his coffee and smiled when I looked up from his notes.

"You can speak freely, Constable," he said. "I won't bite."

"Sir," I said, after a short pause. "Are you dyslexic?"

"Ah, that didn't take you long, did it?" He put his coffee down, stood up, and gestured at the small sofa, coffee table and armchair by the window. "Bring the notes he said. "You might want to spread them out on the table."

I shuffled the papers into my hand, bumping past the commissioner as he asked if I took milk in my coffee.

"No, thank you," I said. I had the notes arranged in page order by the time he came back. I took a pen from my jacket to begin correcting and adjusting the opening paragraph.

"I had a rotten school life," the commissioner said, as he handed me a mug of coffee. He sat down in the armchair as I spread his notes out on the sofa. "The kids called me stupid. I'm sure you can imagine?"

"Yes, Sir," I said, thinking back to the thousands of times I had been called stupid when the words of my country failed me.

"Just arranging all those letters, it's a big puzzle. I learned to do it," he said. "I had to, but it just takes so much time. When they diagnosed me, later in my school years, I was given that time, but you can imagine, in this position, time is in limited supply."

"Yes, Sir," I said, wincing as I burnt my tongue on the coffee.

"So," he said, with a nod to his notes. "What do you think?"

"I can tidy it up, Sir," I said. "It won't take long." I put the mug down and picked up my pen, tucking an errant strand of black hair behind my ear as I leaned over the coffee table.

"You're going to do it now?"

"Yep," I said, scratching a few notes on the first page before moving on to the other.

The commissioner sat quietly for a moment, then got up to answer a call from the phone at his desk. When he was finished, so was I.

"That's fast work, Constable."

"Yes, Sir," I said. And then, without thinking, I pushed my luck a little, blurring the lines between being helpful and sucking up to the boss. "I can do it again, if you need help another time."

The words were already out there, before I bit my lip, wishing I had said nothing at all.

The commissioner smiled, and said, "I'd like that, Constable. And if we could keep it between us?"

"Of course," I said.

"It's not an issue, but I am new, after all. I need

to make an impression."

"Yes, Sir," I said, working hard to suppress a smile. "I know what you mean."

"Good," he said, with a nod to the door. "I won't keep you any longer."

I took that as my cue to leave, but he called me back just as I reached the door.

"One more thing, Constable."

"Yes?"

"Could you pick up that phone on the way out. The one that's been beeping all morning."

"Yes, Sir."

I nodded once, tucked my hair around my ear, and then walked between the workstations of the outer office, weaving between chairs and hip-high filing cabinets, before reaching the phone at the end of the room. I had to move assorted papers, stuffing them on top of more papers inside a dusty box from the copy room, before I found the telephone. I pulled out the chair, dragging it a short way on three wheels – the fourth was missing. I perched on the desk instead, lifted the receiver, and answered the call.

"I'm sorry," I said, after the first gush of words through the line. "If you could repeat that in Danish?"

"Is that *Missing Persons*?"

"Ah," I said, stumbling. "It's the administrative office. Does that help?"

"But this *is* the Missing Persons desk?"

I pressed the handset to my ear, frowning at the rush of static, like wind on the line, as I turned up the volume.

"Yes," I said. "It could be."

"I've been waiting," said the man on the other end of the line. The wind died down for a moment, helping me identify his gender.

"Yes," I said. I turned as the commissioner stepped out of his office and walked towards me. "And how can I help you?"

"I need to report a missing person."

I tugged the pen from my jacket, pinched a piece of paper from out of the box, and waited for the man to give me the details.

"And that last bit," I said, scribbling more notes beside the first few lines I had deciphered. "If you could give me that one more time?"

I wrote the telephone number down beside the address, noting that the man was ringing from the village store, and that if I called back, I should stay on the line while they fetched him.

"I'll do that," I said. "But just one thing." I caught the commissioner's eye as he sipped coffee beside me. "Just hang on, if you could," I said.

"*Aap.*"

"Right, that last bit, one more time, to make sure I got it right. How long did you say the boy has been missing?"

"Twelve months."

"It's been a long time."

"*Aap,*" the man said, adding one more thing before he ended the call.

The commissioner waited as I made a few last notes.

"Dust," he said, as I looked up.

"Sir?"

"On your jacket." He put his mug down and brushed a film of dust from my sleeve.

"Thank you."

"And the call, Constable?"

"Yes," I said. I could feel the pinch of a frown just above my nose. Atii said it was cute, one of my endearing features, but I knew it was often a sign of frustration. Sometimes, more often than I liked to admit, my frowns revealed a sudden spark of interest. The commissioner recognised it at once.

"Are you going to tell me about that call, Constable?"

"Yes, Sir," I said. "But first, I have to ask, do we have a Missing Persons Desk?"

"Well," the commissioner said with a glance at the broken chair and the dusty surface of the desk. "I suppose we do now."

Part 4

Lots of people go missing in Greenland. But reporting a missing person was usually something done locally. Often, the missing person would turn up a day or two later, caught out in bad weather, or delayed by better weather and good hunting that prolonged a trip. Delay was part of daily life in Greenland, and a few days either side of an expected arrival was often nothing more than a slight disappointment, and a good reason to make the most of a person's visit once they did arrive.

Children, lone hunters and fishermen were a different matter, especially when the weather was worse than usual, the temperatures lower, the winds stronger. The opposite was true too, when the ice broke up earlier than usual due to warm winds. People went missing in the south of Greenland, venturing into the mountains, sometimes chasing stray sheep. But all those types of *missing* were often resolved by coordinated searches, sometimes including the Danish Royal Air Force jet with its powerful cameras. The Navy and their helicopters would be brought into the search too. The results varied, of course, just like the weather and the terrain.

"But a Missing Persons *desk*," Atii said, as she bought me a guilty coffee in *Katuaq*, Greenland's

Cultural Centre, just a few convenient strides from the police station. "Having a *desk* is like calling it a department."

I had thought the very same thing. What was needed was more like a cold case department, following up on people who were missing for longer periods of time. In this case, a whole year. What this missing persons case lacked in urgency, it more than made up for with intrigue, something I found particularly appealing.

"Yes," I said, grinning at Atii from behind a tall mug of latte. She looked so much better than the last time I saw her, and yet, at the end of a long day, we both had wayward strands of hair tickling our cheeks, but Atii's clear eyes and lack of vomit was a serious improvement.

"You have a desk, Petra," she said.

"I suppose I do."

It wasn't much of a desk, and it was quickly moved out of the main office, and into a smaller, darker space tucked underneath a staircase. Sergeant Duneq arranged it, assuring the commissioner that the existing telephone line would be hooked up and routed to the new location of Greenland's Missing Persons desk. He made a point of relocating the broken chair too. But it was the desk that made all the difference.

That word again – *desk*.

Like a whole department, all to myself.

Of course, the dust I cleaned from the desk returned two-fold, together with the grit and fine sand from the soles of my colleagues' boots as they tramped up and down the staircase. Even on that very first day, just half an hour after settling me into my new *office*, Sergeant Duneq called a meeting in the small storage space at the top of the stairs. He said it was the only place he could find to meet at such short notice, now that the work schedules had to be revised to accommodate Constable Jensen's trip to Qaanaaq. My colleagues and I clumped together, leaning in and bending with the sharp angles of the roof pressing the team together. It was agreed that the next meeting would be held in the normal place – much larger and often empty – as the potential hazing of a new constable wasn't worth the discomfort. I mouthed a silent word of thanks to the older constable who suggested it, and then did my best to avoid catching the eye of Sergeant Duneq.

My desk was, of course, covered in grit and dust when I returned to it, something Sergeant Duneq noticed with more than a little glee.

"You'll have to do something about that," he said, with another meaty smile. "When you get back."

I waited for him to leave, cleaned my desk, and then pulled it a little further from the stairs, before checking my notes. Ordinarily, I learned, there would have to be more evidence to warrant an officer being sent all the way to the top of Greenland to investigate a case that was over twelve months old, especially when the local constable had been told nothing about it. But a special flight of politicians was already scheduled, in anticipation of the next general election, and the commissioner had reserved me a seat on the flight.

"If you're going to start treading on people's toes – which you will, in this position," he said, on a follow-up visit to see what had become of the desk that had been unearthed earlier that day. "Then you may as well do it in style. And," he said, lowering his voice, "you can keep an ear out for any rumblings from the politicians on board the flight."

"I don't speak Greenlandic," I said.

"And neither do I. So, no better no worse, but you've got your head screwed on right. I trust your intuition, Constable."

"Yes, Sir," I said.

He looked at his watch. "Your flight leaves tomorrow morning. Have one of the patrol cars drop you off at the airport."

I nodded, gathered my notes, and then called Atii the minute the commissioner was gone.

"Coffee," I said. "As soon as your shift's over."

Part 5

The month of May is a perfect time to fly in Greenland. There is plenty of snow to add sharp accents and shadows to the granite peaks, and the warm sun means that you can get away with travelling light. Not that I intended to spend much time out of doors. Once I interviewed the old man in Qaanaaq, once I *humoured* him, then I imagined I would spend the rest of the time indoors, listening to the politicians canvas the residents of Qaanaaq inside the sports hall, the school's Aula, or both. The thought amused me, as did the banter between the politicians on the flight. I chatted with one of them, a slim woman called Nivi Winther. Some people said she was tipped for the top post, if her party won the election, and the seven minutes we chatted together confirmed it for me, and I was convinced she would get my vote. But when her colleagues – all of them male – drew her away to discuss more important matters than a young female police constable might fathom, I noticed something else about Nivi Winther. Behind her natural empathy, there was fire in her bones, and I realised how important it would be for her to lead my country, to give women like me a stronger voice.

"I enjoyed talking to you, Constable," she said, as she left. "I'll leave you to your work."

I checked my notes from Nuuk to Ilulissat, took a coffee break and several rounds of *Candy Crush* on the next hop to Upernavik, and listened to music as we descended to land. And then, back in the air, once I finished staring at the vibrant browns of the exposed mountains, and the deepest of blues and brilliant white crusts of the sea ice, I took another look at my notes, scant though they were.

According to the man on the static line from Qaanaaq, a boy, Isaja Qisuk, went missing in May the previous year. He was seven years old. His birthday was May 14th which meant he would be almost nine by the time I arrived in Qaanaaq. The only other details I had, apart from the caller's contact details, included mention of a narwhal tooth.

The tooth of the narwhal comes in many sizes, a twist of creamy ivory as thick as a man's fist, or as slender as a woman's finger. They can be long, often as tall as a seven-year-old boy, or longer still – perhaps the length of one of those cheap and tiny cars that had become popular in Greenland's capital. A hunter could easily sell a narwhal tooth to a Dane for a couple of thousand Danish kroner. Or he could carve tiny pieces of it into jewellery and make even more money. They are as valuable as they are mystical, and the romantic part of me liked to think the narwhal tooth played an important part in my first missing persons case. The old man in Qaanaaq had assured me that it did.

"It's a double tooth," he'd said when we spoke. "Twisting out of the cranium. Rare and expensive."

The line had crackled beyond coherency before

I could press more information out of him, leaving me to wonder about the connection between the boy and tooth.

The whine and shudder of the undercarriage dropping into position encouraged me to finish the last dregs of my coffee, tuck my notes into my small backpack, and tighten my seatbelt. We landed a few minutes later, bumping onto Qaanaaq's gravel landing strip with a rush of wind pummelling the air brakes. I resisted the urge to clap, smiled at the politicians who couldn't help themselves, and then looked out of the window at the tiny airport building, the flat land tapering down to the sea ice, and the long hump like a beast's back that was Herbert Island, to the south and west of Qaanaaq.

I waited for the politicians to file out of the long tubular cabin of Air Greenland's Dash-7, grabbed my backpack from beneath my seat, and joined them. The local police officer, a tall young Greenlander with pale skin and blond hair called Constable Innarik Umeerinneq greeted me and took me to one side.

"I have to stay with them," he said, nodding at the politicians.

"You know why I'm here?"

"*Aap.* But you'll find nothing. I've been here for four months. No one has said a word about the boy."

"Isaja," I said.

"Yeah, I know." Innarik waved to the politicians that he was ready, apologised once more, and then suggested I try and get a lift into town. "The patrol car's full of politicians," he said. "I'm sorry. I can try and send someone back for you."

"I'll manage," I said.

"It's four kilometres," Innarik said, as he slipped away.

The commissioner had said I would be treading on toes, but Innarik seemed more stressed than irritated. I watched him leave, tugging my backpack onto my shoulder before walking out of the airport.

I blinked in the sun, lifting my hand to shield my eyes the second I left the building. The patrol car was the second to last car to leave the gravel parking lot, disappearing in a cloud of dust, not unlike that which covered my desk back in Nuuk. I waved at a small man leaning against the passenger door of an old pickup truck. He waved back and I walked towards him.

"I know why you're here," he said in Danish, as I approached.

"Excuse me?"

"You've come about the boy."

"Are you the man I talked to on the phone? Aluusaq?"

The man chuckled, laughter lines wrinkling the skin either side of his eyes. He had the thickest grey hair I had ever seen, short, apart from an even thicker tuft, banded at the top of his head as if he was sprouting. His hands were like warm leather as he shook mine. They were the same colour as his coffee-coloured t-shirt, the hem of which hung loosely over the waistband of his jeans. The white bristles on his chin, together with his grey hair, made me think he was at least seventy, but the flash of light in his brown eyes shed years off his tiny body.

"My name is Tuukula," he said. "And I am going to be your guide."

Part 6

Tuukula was not alone. A small girl clambered out of the passenger seat, wedging herself in the tiny space between the driver's seat and the ribbed metal wall of the cab as I got in. The door creaked open and shut, and the hiss of the suspension as I sat down pricked the skin above my nose into a wrinkle. The girl wrinkled her own nose as if she were my mirror, but when I turned to say hello, she disappeared further into the space behind Tuukula's seat, tugging the collar of her pink t-shirt up and over her nose.

"That's Luui," he said, as he got in.

"Who is she?" I asked, tilting my head to get a better look at her. The smudges of dirt on her cheeks hid the freckles beneath them, just as she hid her eyes behind the splayed fingers of her dirty hands. She had the same thick hair as Tuukula, the same intelligent eyes, and totally disarming smile which I saw, when Tuukula started the engine and jerked the pickup into gear.

"Is she your granddaughter?"

Tuukula shook his head. "My daughter," he said, grinning when he finally crunched the gearstick into reverse. "Five years old tomorrow," he said. "We're having a *kaffemik*. You're invited."

"Oh, I'm sorry," I said. "I'll be leaving this

evening on the plane."

"I don't think so," Tuukula said, shaking his head as he bumped the pickup out of the parking space and pointed the nose towards Qaanaaq. He took a pair of sunglasses from the dashboard – the aviator kind – and reached behind his seat to tickle Luui. "Ready?" he shouted, in English.

"Ready steady," she shouted back, followed by a deep breath and the word "*Go,*" shouted at the top of her tiny lungs. Tuukula stomped on the gas pedal and spun the pickup out of the parking lot around the first curve, and into the straight line heading towards the village of Qaanaaq.

Four kilometres, I thought, as I reached for the seatbelt. I tried to click it into the buckle twice before giving up. I closed my eyes for a moment. The sound of the grit and gravel peppering the underside of the car, the side panels and the windscreen forced me to open them again.

"Do you think you could slow down?" I said, grabbing for the handle above the passenger door.

"*Aap,*" Tuukula said, before reaching for Luui's hand, teasing her out of her hiding place and into his lap. Luui took the wheel and Tuukula gave her his sunglasses, holding on to the ends that poked a full finger-length over her ears.

"*Ukaleq,*" Luui said, pointing at a blur of white fur racing across the road ahead of us. Tuukula slammed on the brakes and I braced my hand on the dashboard as Luui slewed the pickup to a stop. The dust cloud enveloped us, as father and daughter stared through the window. Luui lifted the sunglasses from her head, looked at me and then stabbed a tiny finger against the glass. "Ukaleq."

"Yes," I said, relieved that we had stopped. "An Arctic hare."

"And ptarmigan," Tuukula said, pointing further up the mountainside at a flush of white feathers.

"Yes. I see them."

He turned the engine off. Luui continued to drive, adding motor noises of her own, as her father shifted in his seat to look at me.

"I told Aluusaq not to call you. But he is getting old. He wants to find Isaja before he dies." Tuukula bobbed his head as if he was weighing the decision in his mind before answering the old man. "I told him I would help him, if that's what he wanted, but that it would be difficult. It would be hard on him. You understand?"

"Maybe," I said.

"I told him that maybe Isaja doesn't want to be found. And if he did, then maybe Aluusaq wouldn't like what he had to tell him. But Aluusaq feels very bad. So, you are here, and I am here to guide you."

"I don't understand," I said. "You're going to guide me?"

"*Aap.*"

"Where to?"

"To find Isaja."

"Then you know where he is?"

Tuukula shook his head. "*Naamik.*"

Maybe it was the long flight, the take-offs and the landings, to which I could add the madcap race along the gravel road to Qaanaaq, but the puzzle of Isaja's disappearance was now murkier than ever.

"But if you can find him," I said. "Why haven't you looked before?"

Tuukula frowned as he looked at me. "Because he didn't want to be found."

"I don't understand."

"We'll talk later," he said, brushing Luui's hair flat against her head before kissing her cheeks. "Ready?" he whispered, reaching for the key in the ignition.

"Steady," she said.

I gripped the handle above the door and jammed my feet on either side of the footwell.

"*Go*," Luui shouted, and we launched down the gravel road.

Part 7

The dust settled in smoky clouds around the pickup when Tuukula parked outside a small wooden cabin close to the sea ice. Luui took my hand, tugging me over the gearstick and out of the driver's door as her father held it open. I clambered out of the pickup and onto the gravel road, reaching inside the cab for my backpack as Luui made cartoon cartwheels with her stumpy legs, jerking my fingers impatiently and not letting go.

"I'm coming," I said, slipping my backpack over my shoulder as I followed Luui to the front door of the cabin.

There was more dust inside; the musty air sparkled with it. Luui tugged me across the floor and parked me in a padded armchair. The wooden arms were visible at the ends where idle fingers had tugged and teased at old upholstery. Luui chattered away in the Qaanaaq dialect, wholly unconcerned whether or not I answered, she was too busy arranging her meagre selection of toys, mostly plastic horses of various sizes, placing them on my knees, my thighs and in the folds of my jacket hanging over my lap. Tuukula grinned from the doorway to the tiny kitchen off the main room. I heard the *dunk dunk* of water bubbling out of a plastic jerry can as he prepared tea.

"Will we see Aluusaq soon?" I asked, brushing at the dirt on Luui's cheek as she crawled into my lap.

"Tomorrow," Tuukula said.

"About that," I said. "I don't think you heard me earlier."

"I heard you."

"Then perhaps you misunderstood." I lowered my voice as Tuukula appeared in the doorway. "I leave on the same plane later tonight – together with the politicians."

"*Naamik*," he said.

"Why not?"

"Because you have come all this way."

"Yes."

"But there is further to go."

"To find Isaja?"

"*Aap*." Tuukula ducked back into the kitchen as the kettle boiled. He returned with an enamel mug, chipped around the rim, and steaming with the pungent aroma of orange and winter spices. "Christmas tea," he said, pressing the mug into my hands. "I drink it all year round."

I nodded my thanks, holding the mug out of the way as Luui curled up on her side, tucking her knees to her chest and sticking a grubby thumb between wet lips.

"She's tired," Tuukula said.

"I can see that."

"She was up early, waiting for you."

"Why?"

"Because Aluusaq told her they were sending a policeman from Nuuk."

"Police *officer*," I said.

"*Aap*." Tuukula reached down to part Luui's hair with gnarled fingers. "She's excited about finding her brother."

"Isaja is her brother?"

Tuukula nodded. "Her big brother. She remembers him, asks about him all the time."

I felt the pinch of my frown and let it sit there as I processed the new information. Tuukula chuckled, and said, "I am not Isaja's father."

"But you are Luui's?"

"I am."

"Then who is Isaja's father? Aluusaq?"

"He is Isaja's grandfather. His *ata*."

Tuukula brushed the dust from the cover of a cushion before sitting down in the threadbare chair opposite me. The air sparkled between us, and I turned to look out of the sea-crusted panes of glass, just as a gaggle of small boys tumbled past with a football. When I turned back Tuukula was smiling, then sipping his tea, brushing a strange object, like a clear leather sac the size of his palm, hanging from a long length of fishing line from the ceiling.

"How is the tea?" he asked.

"It's good," I said. "Surprisingly, good. I usually drink coffee."

"Latte?"

"Yes." I laughed. "How did you know?"

Tuukula batted the skin sac to one side and it pendulumed slowly between us, defying gravity in long, slow arcs. "The clothes you wear…"

"It's my uniform," I said, slightly mesmerised by the arc of the beige and veined sac.

"The *way* you wear your uniform," he said. "Your hair. The smartphone in your pocket." Tuukula shrugged as I instinctively pressed my palm to my jacket pocket. "These things, make you look like someone who drinks latte." Tuukula smiled as he raised his mug in a gentle toast. "I drink tea."

Luui twitched in my lap as she snored, stretching her legs – longer than they first appeared – over the finger-bitten arm of the chair. I lifted my arm and held my tea above her leg, while stroking her gritty hair with my free hand.

"You said Isaja is her brother?"

"Was," Tuukula said. "I believe Isaja is dead."

Part 8

I have always considered myself Greenlandic. Even in my darkest moments, when the older children teased me at school, calling me the *Danish girl*, I would look at my skin, often darker than theirs with their Danish genes, my long jet black hair and my fierce brown, almost black eyes hard as hazelnuts, cracking with conviction that I *was* Greenlandic. That I *am* Greenlandic. But in that tiny wooden cabin, just a stone's throw from the sea ice, dust clinging to my boots and a small child snoring in my lap, I questioned my identity, wondered what I was missing, why the so-called simple life of the hunter and his family confounded me so.

Tuukula caught the query in my eyes and laughed softly. He finished his tea, stood up, and quietly plucked the enamel mug from my hands, saying, "More tea. There is much to tell."

Luui slept in my lap, and I brushed her hair at each twitch of her limbs, wondering when I might return to Nuuk, when I was expected. One thought did make me smile, as I pictured Sergeant Jowls scowling at the duty roster, perhaps even taking an extra shift to cover for the girl for whom training was very much over.

"You're smiling," Tuukula said, as he pressed the handle of a fresh mug of tea into my hand, the dried orange together with the thin black leaves of herbs and tea pricked the insides of my nose.

"Yes."

"That's good," he said. "It's important to be comfortable before a long tale. Are you comfortable?" Tuukula gestured at his daughter.

"I think my legs are asleep," I said, with a glance at Luui. She had her father's nose, slightly bent, but less gnarly. "I'm fine," I said. "Tell me about Isaja."

"Isaja," Tuukula said, as he sat down, "was a curious boy with a quick mind." Tuukula tapped his head with the middle finger of his right hand, a thimble-length shorter than it was supposed to be. I wondered if he lost the tip in a hunting accident, but he interrupted that thought with a description of Isaja: tall for his age, thin hair, but wiry black like his skin, darker than many of the other children. "His quick mind made him quick with his fists. He had to be. Children can be wicked."

"Yes," I said, thinking back to my own schooling in Nuuk, and the dark winter nights in the children's home, when emotions were charged, running on rocket fuel.

"The teachers called him difficult, but what did they know?" Tuukula shook his head. "Nothing. But Aluusaq, *he* knew. *His* genes. Trace them all the way back to the explorers, that black man who came with Peary? More smarts," Tuukula said, with another stubby tap of his finger to his head. "Aluusaq's son, Isaja's father, was a bad man."

"Was?"

"He's gone," Tuukula said, with a curt nod of

his head. "Rassi left after a fight."

"Sounds like there's a lot of fighting here," I said.

"Only when people are drunk. But Rassi drank a lot, and Isaja spent a lot of time with his *ata*. But he loved his father all the same. For when Rassi was sober he was a great hunter. He had the eye," Tuukula said, pressing his stubby finger to his right eye. "He could spot narwhal from far away, see the tusks fencing in the water, parting the smoke, the condensation, you know? He was always the first into the water. His *qajaq* was always strapped to his sledge, or on his boat, when they sledged the boats to the edge of the ice. Rassi was the fastest in a *qajaq*. He did everything better and faster than everyone else."

"Including drinking?" I asked.

"*Aap.*"

Tuukula fell silent as he curled his hand around the skin sac. He pinched the fishing line between finger and thumb and tugged the line from the tack securing it to the wooden rafters in the ceiling. The sac darkened in Tuukula's hand, as if filling with rich smoke the colour of chocolate, or blood. I stared at the sac, now dark, in his palm, curious at the smile on his face. But the smile turned, the lines of his mouth flattened, and he burst the sac in his hand. I flinched, expecting smoke, but seeing just the shadow of Tuukula's skin blocking the light from the sac.

"Magic," he said, and the light from the fjord blistered through the salt crystals webbing the glass, tickling the sheen of his eye. "I can do tricks, but

Isaja tried to perform the greatest trick of all."

Luui stirred at her brother's name. She tilted her head, casting a sleepy glance at my face, before resting again, heavy lids closing on young eyes.

"What did he do?" I asked. "What trick?"

I forgot all about taking notes. Tuukula's illusion with the skin sac, and his description of Isaja and his father, Rassi the hunter, hooked me with words and images of thick ice, black smoking seas, and tusked whales.

"Isaja knew that when his father caught a narwhal, the whale was butchered, the squares of skin – *Mattak* – shared, then only the tooth remained. As soon as Rassi sold the tooth, the drinking would begin. The day Isaja went missing, Rassi came home with a double tooth, two tusks from the same whale. Rare? Yes," he nodded. "And worth more than double the price of a single tooth. Isaja knew a little magic – he had watched me often enough – and he thought he could do magic that night. He thought he could make the double tooth disappear."

"You mean he stole it?" I said, as the image of a young boy racing through the gravel streets, cradling two white tusks taller than he was, flitted through my mind.

"Isaja did not steal the teeth," Tuukula said. "His magic backfired. Not only did the teeth disappear, but so did Isaja."

"That's when he went missing?"

Tuukula nodded. "Almost twelve months ago to this day."

Part 9

I expected the light to fade, but the warm yellows and burnt orange rays of the spring Arctic sun, bathed the mountains and shone from the glass and aluminium chimney stacks of the houses in Qaanaaq late into the night. I missed the political rally, the Q&A in the sports hall, and the barbecue seal that followed. I also missed my flight, hearing the heavy buzz of the De Havilland Dash 7's four propellers cutting through the thick evening air. Tuukula gently lifted Luui from my lap sometime later in the early evening, laying her in her tiny bed beside his in the room next to the kitchen. He showed me the bathroom bucket, when I asked, and then made more tea, drinking it outside as I freshened up with a bowl of cool water. I joined Tuukula outside on a sun-bitten bench as he smoked a hand-rolled cigarette.

"One a day," he said, flicking ash from the cigarette. "Sometimes two if I'm travelling."

"You were telling me about the day Isaja disappeared," I said, as I sat down beside him. The old wood creaked under our combined weight, bringing a smile to Tuukula's lips.

"It was a night like this," he said, waving his hand towards the ice edge, as if brushing the coast with his fingertips. "There were seven sledges. The

39

hunters had caught three narwhals. They butchered them far out on the ice." Tuukula grinned. "They would have had a hell of a time keeping the dogs in check, all that meat, the stink of blood. They would be going crazy. But they can't run on full bellies. The hunters fed them once they got back. Isaja stood there," Tuukula said, pointing to a gap between two grey frames of wood. "His father's drying racks. He waited there. He had that shuffle that kids do when they are half excited and half scared. Something good is coming, they know that, the whole town talks about it. But there is always a downside." Tuukula pinched the end of his cigarette, flaking the last paper and tobacco into the grit and dust at his feet. "Isaja saw his father. He waved. And then he saw the tusks."

"You saw Isaja that night?" I asked.

"*Aap.*" Tuukula pointed. "Standing right there."

"And you saw where he went? After that?" I pulled my notebook from my pocket, turning to a fresh page as Tuukula spoke.

"Isaja helped his father with the dogs. He put each of them on the chain. Isaja's mother," Tuukula said, with a brief smile. "Is Luui's mother too. She helped carry the meat. More people helped. There were a lot of people." Tuukula traced his hand over imaginary heads in front of where we sat. "That was when Isaja disappeared. I didn't think anything of it. But he was gone, and so were the teeth." Tuukula turned slightly to face me, his bony knees bumping mine. "This is the interesting part, the real magic. Isaja took the teeth."

"Yes," I said. "Both of them."

"That's right. But maybe you haven't seen narwhal teeth?"

"I have," I said, thinking about the creamy ivory tusks I had seen in the souvenir shops in Nuuk, and the giant tusks, dry, flaked and cracked behind glass in the museum. "They are all sizes."

"And some are taller than we are." Tuukula nodded. "But a hunter will bring back the head of a narwhal, cut flat, standing up with the teeth pointing into the sky, still attached." Tuukula bent his left arm at right angles, tapping his elbow with the stub of his right index finger. "Imagine the head, here, about the size of two small tyres and just as heavy. Then the teeth," he said, tracing his finger up his arm. "Taller than Isaja." Tuukula relaxed and reached for his tea. "Real magic," he said. "Better than mine, for how else can a seven-year-old boy carry a narwhal head with a double tusk off the beach and out of the village?"

"He had help?" I said.

"Maybe he did." Tuukula shrugged. "But no one saw him or the teeth again." Tuukula tipped his head back and swallowed the last dregs of his tea. "I'm getting old," he said, the late sun twinkled in his eye and cast a warm glow on his wrinkled face. "I drink to keep me lubricated, and the more I drink, the more I have to pee, which keeps me moving." Tuukula grinned as he stood up. "You can sleep in my bed. I'll sleep on the couch."

"I can stay at the hotel," I said.

"Closed," he said. "For the spring. You can have my bed." Tuukula burped and patted his chest. "Luui creeps under the covers in the early morning.

Just so you know. Kiss her head and hold her hand and she falls right asleep." The light caught his eye again as he chuckled. "She farts," he said.

"Okay," I said, frowning at the curious detail. "That's good to know."

I checked my smartphone for messages as Tuukula stretched his legs, weaving between the drying racks on his way to the sea ice. It occurred to me that my usual city girl sensibilities had been disarmed, as if they had been turned off by the gentle and intimate family nature of Tuukula and his young daughter. I felt adopted, almost, and I discovered a gentle warmth flooding through my body as I sat in the glow of the High Arctic sun, texting Atii that I was roughing it, and that she would have to do without me for a few more days. In truth, I had no idea how many.

Part 10

Luui pressed her knee into my nose as she crawled out of bed, dragging the duvet with her as if it was an oversized comfort blanket. I sighed, rubbed the sleep from my eyes and dressed, blinking into the morning sun, curious that it should be so strong already. Clearly, I wasn't quite prepared for spring in the far north of Greenland. I dressed quickly and quietly, draping my heavy police jacket over the back of the armchair as I padded through the living room, following the sounds of Luui's excited chatter into the kitchen. I caught the word *six* in my limited Greenlandic and remembered that it was her birthday.

"I need to talk to Aluusaq today," I said, as Tuukula pressed a cup of coffee into my hand.

"It's black, unless you want long-life milk," he said, with a nod to a tiny fridge shuddering in the corner.

"Black is fine," I said. Luui curled one hand into mine, tugging me to one of two seats pressed up against the wall. The kitchen table lay flat, hinged against the wall with robust screws of assorted sizes and heads. Luui pushed my knees to one side with grubby palms, turning me away from the table until she could lift it and prop it up with a square leg of wood. I put my coffee down on the surface as Luui beamed at me. "Aluusaq," I said, as Tuukula cracked eggs into a frying pan. "Where can I find him?"

"Luui will take you," he said. "I need time to tidy up and bake the cakes for her *kaffemik*."

"*Kaffemik!*" Luui said, twirling in the tiny space between me and the electric hob where Tuukula fried the eggs. She twirled into my legs, bumping the table with her head, before crawling into my lap with her hand pressed to her temple.

"Let me see," I said, peeling away her fingers to blow on her forehead. Luui laughed and I blew some more, pushing her hair one way and then the other until Tuukula clicked his fingers and pointed at the bathroom door. Luui slipped off my lap and disappeared into the bathroom.

"She has to wash," Tuukula said. "Then I'll fix her hair, find a dress and send her with you to Aluusaq."

"Her grandfather?"

"*Naamik*." Tuukula shook his head. "Aluusaq was Rassi's father, Isaja's *ata*."

I checked my notes as Tuukula slid a plate onto the table – fried egg with mushrooms from a glass jar, heaped on top of a piece of square toast, buttered thickly. He served three helpings, then called for Luui to hurry before sitting down opposite me. Luui crawled onto Tuukula's lap, reaching between his arms for a fork. I smiled at the sight of father and daughter eating, with four arms, two mouths and a lot of wriggling; Luui bounced as she ate.

Tuukula picked at a knot in Luui's hair, then

sent her back into the bathroom to clean her teeth. I
stood up, fixed my ponytail, and then left Tuukula
at the table. I knocked on the bathroom door and as
I opened it I saw Luui standing on an upturned crate
while brushing her teeth. I leaned around her,
pulling my own toothbrush and paste from my
pocket. She held up her brush and I squeezed a fat
worm of paste onto it. Luui's eyes widened as she
tasted it. When Luui finished brushing her teeth, she
stared at me in the mirror taped to the wall, and I
stood behind her, teasing her hair into long, smooth
lengths with a brush I found beside the mug of
toothbrushes and wrinkled tubes of toothpaste.

"How about a ponytail?" I said, tilting my head
to one side and letting my hair fall over my
shoulder. Luui nodded, plucking at the light blue
sleeves of my police shirt as I found a spare elastic
in my pocket, slipping my fingers through it, before
rolling it to the base of Luui's ponytail. I smiled as
she chattered away, catching less than half of what
she said as the Qaanaaq dialect proved even more
difficult than the West Greenlandic I heard most
days. The consonants were softer, more edible and
swallowed faster than I could fathom.

"Luui," Tuukula called from the kitchen.
"Clothes," he added, in Danish.

"*Aap*," she said, slipping off the crate and
whirling into the kitchen.

I stayed by the mirror, curious at the smile
curling one side of my mouth, as I remembered
another little girl, not unlike Luui; only I couldn't
remember having so much energy when *I* was five.

"Hello," I whispered to my reflection, as I fast-forwarded to the present. "This is the Missing Persons desk. How can I help you?" The truth was I had no idea, but my new job was certainly varied, if a little short on creature comforts. *"You're roughing it, girl,"* I said, in my best imitation of Atii's big-city-girl slang.

"Luui's waiting outside," Tuukula said, as I thanked him for breakfast. "Bring her back at two o'clock."

"Tuukula," I said. "I'm investigating Isaja's disappearance, not babysitting Luui."

"Aap," he said, eyes twinkling in the early morning light. "Try not to be late."

Part 11

A day later than planned and one day over schedule, Luui led me up a flight of two low steps and onto the bruised wooden deck of a white-walled house. Flaps of bitumen at the corners of the roof waved in the wind coming off the ice cap, sending a chill past my collar and down my neck, cooling my irritation at Tuukula – using me to look after his daughter – as my curiosity was piqued. Luui rapped her tiny knuckles on the door, reached up for the handle and stepped inside Aluusaq's house. I followed, pressing toe to heel as I removed my boots, in a similar action to Luui. I heard her greet Aluusaq as I tugged my notebook from my jacket pocket, before stepping into the living room. The thin old man hunched and folded into a lawn chair was not who I had expected.

Aluusaq's eyes were charcoal grey when they should have been dark brown. His skin, parched and crevassed like a dried fish, was brittle to the touch when I shook his hand. He nodded to the chair beside him and I sat down as Luui settled on the couch. Aluusaq spoke softly, as if his words were blowing from off the ice cap, like the wind, but warmer as he expressed his surprise that I was sitting in his living room, actively investigating the case of his missing grandson.

"The local police would look into it if you asked them," I said.

"They have, and they found nothing," Aluusaq said, the words rattling out of his thin frame. "When I called Nuuk, I asked specifically for the Missing Persons desk. I knew they would have to respond, and now you're here."

He said something to Luui, waving vaguely in the direction of the kitchen, while I wondered how much I should tell him, about how little he could expect, especially twelve months after Isaja went missing.

"Why did you wait so long to report him missing?" I asked.

"I didn't. I reported it straight away. But Rassi said Isaja was hiding, and that he would be back soon. I wanted to believe my son."

"And now?"

Aluusaq wiped at his cheek, although his eyes seemed too dry for tears. He smiled at Luui as she returned from the kitchen, the tip of her tongue clamped between her lips, as she carried two glasses of water, clogged with ice beneath the lip of each glass. Her shoulders sagged as I took one of the glasses, and she reached up to Aluusaq with the second. Luui scurried back into the kitchen before I could thank her. I sipped the water, frowning slightly at the hint of cold salt on my lips.

"From the sea," Aluusaq said. "The children bring me ice from the icebergs to cool my drinks. Luui knows where I keep it." Aluusaq smiled again. "You only taste the salt once."

"Yes," I said, putting my glass down. "You said

Rassi said Isaja was just hiding?"

"*Aap.*"

"For how long did you believe him?"

Aluusaq wiped a second time at his cheek. Several breaths rattled in and out of his lungs before he spoke. "A long time," he said, quietly. "Too long."

"Did Rassi visit you during that time?"

"Once a week. Sometimes more if he needed money."

"And you asked him about Isaja?"

"Every time."

"And what did he say?"

"That he was staying with friends or living with his mother."

"And was he?"

"Isaja's mother lives in Ilulissat. I don't know her number."

Aluusaq looked out of the south-facing window, and I imagined him staring as far as Ilulissat, searching for his grandson. If I had known that Isaja's mother was in Ilulissat, I might have stopped on the way.

"He's not there," Aluusaq said. "Not in Ilulissat."

"How can you be sure?"

"I can't, but no one remembers Isaja leaving. That's the only thing everybody agrees on, when they talk about him. They are talking about him again, now that you have come." Aluusaq caught my eye, staring at me, searching for something with the same intense gaze he had when staring south in search of his grandson. "They think you have come to arrest me."

"Why would they think that?"

"Because," Aluusaq said, brushing his dry cheeks with a crooked finger, "they know what everybody knows, that Isaja is dead."

"And why do they think I've come to arrest you?"

"Because before my son died, he told everyone in Qaanaaq that I killed Isaja."

Part 12

"My son was a great hunter," Aluusaq said. He pointed his crooked finger at a picture hanging on the wall, and I walked around the couch to look at it. Aluusaq's words followed me, describing the ghosts in the photograph. "He had the strongest dogs, the fastest *qajaq*, and the keenest eye. He could see…"

"Narwhals fencing at the very edge of the ice," I whispered, my face pressed close to the photograph, as Aluusaq sang the familiar praises of his son. I was curious as to what I should think about Rassi, the great hunter, the great drinker. Twice now, I had heard men complement Rassi on his prowess as a hunter, and both men – Tuukula first, and now Aluusaq – had also described the other Rassi, the one who scared his son so much he fled the village with the double narwhal tooth.

I looked at the man in the photograph, imagining a younger Aluusaq in his stead, with a thick head of black hair, bushy black eyebrows protruding above keen eyes in a sun-beaten face. The boy standing beside Rassi in the photo was no taller than Luui – perhaps the same age when the photo was taken. While Rassi looked straight at the camera, Isaja looked up at his father. There was a depth in the boy's eyes suggesting he had seen too much, and that he could see into the future.

"Isaja was four and half when they took that picture," Aluusaq said.

I made a note in my notebook and returned to sit beside Aluusaq, glimpsing Luui, just visible in the kitchen, playing with a jigsaw puzzle at the kitchen table as I sat down.

"Aluusaq," I said. "What happened to your son?"

The old man gave a slow shrug. "No one knows. He disappeared, like Isaja. People say he went through the ice."

"Where?"

"On the way to Siorapaluk. Fifty kilometres," Aluusaq said, pointing. "To the north and west."

"He was never found?"

"No."

"Then why do people say he went through the ice?"

"Because they found his team. The dogs ran all the way to Siorapaluk."

"Did they search for him?"

"It was mid-winter." Aluusaq shook his head. "Minus fifty. It was crazy to make the journey. The wind was blowing."

"But if it was minus fifty," I said. "Wouldn't the ice be thick?"

"There is one place," Aluusaq said. "Where the ice is always thin. The tide runs quickly there, eating away at the ice in the bay. You can be unlucky," Aluusaq said. "I think Rassi was unlucky."

The old man looked away and I expected him to

wipe at a dry tear on his parched cheeks. But he kept his fingers in his lap, clenched, as if suppressing something.

"But what about his dogs?" I said. "You said they ran all the way to Siorapaluk. They must have crossed the ice."

"He would have cut the sledge from the traces," Aluusaq said. "They came in a fan of dogs. But no sledge."

"This was mid-winter?"

"*Aap.*"

"Earlier this year?"

Aluusaq nodded. "In February."

I sucked at my teeth as I did a quick calculation. It was May. Isaja had been missing for nearly a year. He went missing *last* May, before the ice broke up. But his father, Rassi, didn't die until February the following year, if he died at all.

"Rassi told you Isaja was hiding, or with his mother in Ilulissat," I said, pressing the tip of my pen to a clean page in my notebook. "And you believed him, for ten months, before Rassi went missing. Is that right?"

Aluusaq held my gaze and nodded, just once.

"But before he left, Rassi told people here that you killed his son."

Another nod.

I looked at Aluusaq, curious for a moment as to *how* he might have killed anybody when he couldn't even fetch ice from the sea for his water.

"Ten months after your grandson goes missing," I said, tapping my pen on the page. "Your son goes missing, presumed dead."

"*Aap*," Aluusaq said.

"But you waited three more months before calling the police in Nuuk."

I gripped the pen and the notebook in my hand, reaching for my glass to take a sip of salty water. Aluusaq watched me, waited for me to swallow before he spoke.

"And you want to know why?" he said, as I put down my glass.

"Yes," I said.

Aluusaq glanced at the photograph on the wall before continuing. "I had given up all hope," he said, after a long, rattling breath. "But then something happened that gave me the strength to look again, just one more time, before my time is done."

"And what was that, Aluusaq? What happened?"

Aluusaq paused, and then said, "Somebody tried to sell a narwhal tooth to one of the Danish teachers in Qaanaaq. It was a double tooth."

"Isaja's tooth," I said, with a click of my pen.

"*Aap*," Aluusaq said, and for a moment, his eyes darkened, flooding the sickly grey with a vibrant flush of brown, the same eyes as his son and grandson, the eyes of a hunter.

Part 13

I pressed Aluusaq for more details, but he knew little more, only that a Greenlander tried to sell the tooth to a temporary teacher.

"But you don't know who he is?"

"*Naamik.*"

"What about the name of the teacher?" I asked, but Aluusaq shook his head.

Luui appeared in the doorway. She padded across the floor, slipped her tiny hand into mine, and gave me a gentle but insistent tug. I checked the time on my smartphone and nodded. It was almost two o'clock. Aluusaq nodded when I told him I would be in touch, and again when I said he should contact me if he remembered anything, if he heard anything, or if something new occurred that he thought might be relevant. Confident that I had covered all the bases, I tugged my boots on and stepped out of Aluusaq's house, blinking into the sun and squinting after Luui as she bounded down the steps. She stopped beside the familiar dark blue police Toyota, hands on her hips as she stared up at Constable Umeerinneq.

"Did he tell you anything?" Umeerinneq asked, as I stepped off Aluusaq's deck and joined them in the street.

"Background information," I said.

"About his son disappearing in February?"

"Yes."

"And his grandson in May last year."

"He told me that, and how Rassi said he killed Isaja."

Umeerinneq shook his head. "Aluusaq has been sick for nearly two years now. He's too weak to do much more than sit in that chair. The council has a helper get him up in the morning, make his meals, and put him to bed at night." Umeerinneq shrugged. "Aluusaq didn't kill anybody."

"No," I said. "But he feels responsible." I pulled out my notebook and laid it flat on the bonnet of the patrol car, beckoning for Umeerinneq to come closer as I flipped through the pages. Luui tugged at the cargo pocket of my trousers, and I reached down to hold her hand, saying, "Just a minute," as I pointed at my notes about the man trying to sell the tooth.

"A double tooth?"

"That's what Aluusaq said."

"I never heard about that, but a lot can happen in the winter that just seeps out into the dark. Easy to miss when you're alone," Umeerinneq said.

"But you must know someone who might have tried to sell a tooth?"

"There's this one guy," Umeerinneq said. He took a pen from the sleeve pocket on his jacket, writing a name in block capitals in my notepad. "Peter Ulloriaq," he said. "I can try and rustle him up. Although, I haven't seen him for a few days."

"Hunting?"

"Peter?" Umeerinneq laughed. "No, too lazy.

Plus, he's got a few problems – only one eye and a limp. Left leg, I think." Umeerinneq looked down as Luui tugged once more at my trousers. "You found a friend."

"Yes," I said, slipping my notebook into my jacket pocket. "And it's her birthday. We're late for her *kaffemik*. She's Tuukula's daughter."

"Tuukula?"

"Yes. I stayed there last night."

Umeerinneq caught my eye and then looked away. "Yeah, I'm sorry about that. I should have offered you a place to stay, but I got caught up with the politicians. They kept me busy, and it was late before I remembered you were here."

"It's fine. No problem," I said. "But I think we have to go."

"I'll give you a ride," he said, opening the Toyota's rear passenger door. Umeerinneq said something to Luui and she clambered into the patrol car. He helped her with her seatbelt, shut the door and then gestured for me to get in. "Tuukula is an interesting man," Umeerinneq said, as he started the engine.

"He's a hunter," I said.

"Well, yes, he hunts," Umeerinneq said. "But he's not really a hunter. He's something else."

"What?" I said, as Umeerinneq frowned. "You can't tell me?"

Umeerinneq looked in the rear-view mirror, angling it down to see Luui as he said something in Greenlandic.

"*Angakkoq*," she said. Luui stretched her arm outwards and opened her tiny fist with a flash of fingers. "*Poof*," she said, and then, in English, "Magic."

"Your *ataata* is a magician?" I asked, furrowing my brow with another trademark frown.

"Not a magician," Umeerinneq said. "Tuukula is a shaman."

Part 14

Luui leaped out of the patrol car as soon as Umeerinneq opened the door. She bustled into the crowd of children playing outside the door of her home, grinning as they pressed small coins into her palms, sometimes a bar of chocolate, sometimes something bigger. I realised I had nothing and wondered what I should give.

"People up here give what they can," Umeerinneq said, as if reading my thoughts. "It doesn't have to be much. A few coins, five kroner, maybe twenty. If you give too much," he said, as I pulled a fifty kroner note from my pocket, "it could send the wrong signal."

"I'll give it her later," I said.

"Sure."

Umeerinneq followed me past the children and inside Tuukula's cabin. The chairs were pushed right up to the walls, and a small table – just two crates with a broad plank of grey, flaky wood between them – supported three huge chocolate cakes with sugar frosting, all the more impressive when compared with the meagre surroundings. The cabin smelt of chocolate, coffee and fish, the oiliest fish I could ever remember smelling, or tasting, when Tuukula pressed a Swiss Army knife into my hand and pointed at the fish on the flat cardboard box on the kitchen floor. I cut a thick cube of raw white meat from the flat fish, licking at the oil on my lips, grinning at Tuukula who took the knife from my hand and passed it to one of the other guests. There were four adults and two small children crouched around the fish, and a fourth person, a middle-aged man, sitting on one of the two chairs in the kitchen.

"Peter Ulloriaq," Umeerinneq said, as the man stared at us.

Peter took one look at Umeerinneq, before bolting for the back door.

He moved faster than I expected for a man with a limp. Nor did his limited eyesight slow him down. Peter weaved around the empty oil cans rusting behind Tuukula's cabin, ducked through a gap in the tall picket fence, separating the row of hunting and fishing cabins along the beach front from the water tower and oil tank behind them. Umeerinneq called out for Peter to stop, as I slipped through the picket fence and gave chase.

"I'll get the car," Umeerinneq shouted.

I shouted something back, then pressed my hand around the grip of my pistol, something I instinctively did when running. I chided myself about it, thinking that I should learn how best to wear my belt and holster, then forgot all about it again, as Peter speeded up.

Peter's mistake was trying to climb the gantry running around the water tower, jumping up to reach for the lowest rung of the ladder to pull it down to the ground. I tumbled into him, throwing him off balance and sending a cloud of dust and grit into our hair and faces. Peter spat grit from his mouth as he rolled away from me.

"Stop," I said, brushing strands of gritty hair from my face. "Peter, we just want to talk to you."

Peter scrabbled to his feet, waving me off and staggering down a stony bank back towards the picket fence. I heard the patrol car, stones plinging against the panels, as Umeerinneq sped along the road, blocking Peter's path.

I slowed as Peter leaned, bent double, against the picket fence, chest heaving, hands pressed to his knees. He lifted his chin, glared at me with his one good eye, then spat a stream of dusty phlegm into the dirt.

"I've done nothing wrong," he said, in Danish.

"I know." I stopped just a few metres away, catching my breath, and letting my hands dangle at my sides, keeping them clear of my pistol and cuffs. "But you might know something that can help me find a boy."

"I don't know anything about Isaja."

"Isaja?" I said, as Umeerinneq approached from the other side of Peter. "What do you know about him?"

"Rassi's son?" Peter said. "You're looking for him?" He glanced at Umeerinneq and then spat one more time. "Everyone's talking about it. Ever since Aluusaq made the call to Nuuk. Now you're here."

"That's right," Umeerinneq said. "Now she's here, maybe you can tell her what you never told me, eh?"

"I don't know where the boy is."

"Okay," I said. "But what about the tooth?" I

took a step closer. "Do you know anything about a narwhal tooth?"

"A double tooth," Umeerinneq added.

Peter straightened his back. He nodded as he leaned against the fence. "*Aap*," he said. "I found a tooth, a double tooth, like you say, and I tried to sell it."

"Where did you find it?" I asked.

Peter lifted his hand and straightened a bony finger. He pointed north, and said, "On the way to Siorapaluk."

Part 15

Umeerinneq said he would drive Peter home once he had answered my questions. He described an old derelict hut, located above a small bay on the way to Siorapaluk.

"No one goes there," he said, dusting himself off as I started a fresh page in my notepad.

"Then why did you?"

"I was with Sakiusi, a hunter. We were coming back from Siorapaluk. He said it was a place where polar bears had denned, and he wanted to see if there were any tracks in the area. I was cold. I told him to leave me at the hut."

"And you went inside?"

Peter shook his head. "It's a bad place. I didn't want to go inside."

"So, you didn't see anyone?"

"I waited by the snowmobile for Sakiusi to finish looking."

"But you found a narwhal tooth?"

"*Aap*," Peter said, with a nod. "Wrapped in a plastic tarp, half buried under a pile of rocks, like it was on top of a grave. The wind had blown the snow off it. The tarp was flapping. I took a look, found the tooth – both of them. And then Sakiusi came back."

"And you brought the tooth back to Qaanaaq?"

"*Aap.*" Peter looked at Umeerinneq. "I didn't steal it. I found it."

Peter said nothing more. Umeerinneq nodded at the car, sliding one of the broken slats in the fence to one side as Peter stepped through it.

"I'll catch you later," he said.

I waved, waited until they had driven away, and then walked back to Tuukula's house. There were new faces at the *kaffemik*, filling the cabin with shuffles and a quiet chatter between sawing meat from the fish, and calling for more coffee. Tuukula met me at the back door, grinning as he pointed at two plastic garden chairs just to one side.

"I need a break," he said, as he rolled a cigarette on his knee. "They can get their own coffee."

"How's Luui?"

"How is she, or where is she?"

"Where, I suppose." I slipped my hand in my pocket. "I have something for her."

"Give it to her later," Tuukula said. He lit his cigarette and then lifted his chin, nodding at the picket fence behind us. "What happened with Peter?"

"I thought he could help with the investigation. Aluusaq said a man tried to sell a narwhal tooth, like the one you said Isaja stole from his father."

"He made it disappear," Tuukula said. "There's a difference."

"Okay," I said. "But it's possible that Peter made that same tooth disappear from a cabin further north."

"On the way to Siorapaluk?"

"Yes. You know it?"

"I know where it is."

"Of course, you do," I said.

Tuukula smoked as I wrestled with an idea in my head. I needed to see the cabin, that much was clear, but I was already overdue. A message beeped into my smartphone, and I glanced at it, swiping it to one side as soon as I saw the sender's name.

"A friend?" Tuukula asked.

"My superior, Sergeant Jowls."

"Howls?"

"*Jowls*," I said, laughing as I pretended to pinch rolls of fat around my neck. "His real name is Duneq."

"And what does he want?"

"He says I have to come back to Nuuk."

"Wednesday," Tuukula said. "That's the next flight, weather depending."

I checked the date on my phone, biting my lip as I made my decision.

"I want to see the cabin."

Tuukula raised his eyebrows, just once, then started to roll a second cigarette. "For later," he said, tucking it behind his ear when he was finished.

"Tuukula, did you hear what I said?"

"That you want to go to the hut?" He nodded. "I heard you."

"And?"

He waved as Luui opened the back door. "I think you will find answers there," he said, as Luui bounced across the dirt and into his lap.

"But I don't know how to get there, and even if I did, I don't think my budget will stretch to a helicopter." I laughed at the word *budget* wondering if I even had one.

"But you want to go?"

"I think I owe it to Isaja and his grandfather."

"He won't like what you might find there."

"But you think I'll find something? Don't you?"

"*Aap*," Tuukula said.

"And you know the way?"

"I do."

"Tuukula..."

Luui fidgeted on Tuukula's lap. He brushed her fringe to one side, curled his finger inside her ponytail, and then kissed her on the forehead. Luui leaned against Tuukula's chest, reaching for the cigarette behind his ear, giggling when he swatted at her fingers.

"We will take you," Tuukula said, tickling Luui. She giggled off his lap and he tapped her lightly on the bottom, sending her back into the cabin as a new wave of guests replaced the last.

"*We*?" I said.

"*Aap*, Luui and me. It is a long way, but we have the sun, we can sledge through the night."

"Sledge? You don't have a snowmobile?"

"I do have a snowmobile," Tuukula said.

He pointed at something hidden just behind the oil barrels, and I sighed at the sight of a broken windshield, a bent ski, and a seat that looked like it had been nibbled by a giant mouse.

"Puppies," Tuukula said, when he saw where I was looking. "But now they are grown, and they've grown strong." He stood up, plucked the cigarette from behind his ear, and stuck it between his lips. "I sometimes have two," he said. "When I'm travelling." He lit the cigarette, puffed a small cloud of smoke above his head, and then pointed to the north. "Constable Jensen," he said. "Let's find you some proper clothes. We leave tonight."

Part 16

Luui took my hand and guided me around Tuukula's long, broad sledge, pointing out the different parts, as I fiddled with the straps holding up the polar bear skin trousers Tuukula insisted that I wear. However dishevelled his cabin might appear, the shaman's sledging clothes, gear and dogs seemed to be of the highest quality – to my ignorant eyes, at least. Luui rattled off another string of long Greenlandic words, quite unperturbed at my limited grasp of her language. She started on the dogs next, calling out each name in English. I caught the name of the last two of fifteen dogs as I followed her to the head of the team.

"Cargo?" I asked, pointing at the large white male just behind the lead dog.

"Cargo very bad," Luui said, in English. The ears of her hood wiggled as she shook her head. Her hood had fascinated me earlier, sewn from dog fur with real dog ears, soft and pointed.

"And that one?" I pointed at the lead dog.

"Spirit," Luui said. She took my hand again, skirting around Cargo and pulling me all the way to the head of the team where she promptly let go and pulled Spirit into a generous hug. Cargo growled behind us until the arrival of Umeerinneq's patrol car bumping over the ice foot and onto the sea ice distracted the big sledge dog.

A chill wind followed in the wake of the patrol car and I tugged at the collar of my sealskin smock, pulling the hood over my head as Umeerinneq stepped out of the car.

"I can guess where you're headed and I don't suppose I can stop you," he said, as he walked across the ice.

"The answers are at the cabin," I said. "Everything points in that direction."

"There's trouble in that direction, too." Umeerinneq paused at a shout from Tuukula, calling for Luui to help him. "It's May. The ice might be thick here, but further up the coast, where the tide is stronger, it will be weaker, more dangerous."

"I'll be fine," I said, brushing my hair to one side as the wind caught it.

"Okay," Umeerinneq said. "But just one more thing – your boss called."

"The commissioner."

"No." He frowned. "The other one. Sergeant Duneq. He wanted me to remind you that you don't have a budget for this, and that you are overstepping your authority."

"Did he say training was over, too?"

"What?"

"Nothing," I said. Nuuk felt very far away, and the sergeant's words seemed less weighty than usual. I felt a surge of giddiness at the thought that I was beyond the sergeant's reach, tempered only by the butterflies in my stomach at the thought of sledging north across thin ice, towards Siorapaluk.

"Constable?" Tuukula said.

I started at the sound of his voice, wondering how he could move so quietly. He pointed at Luui sitting on a canvas kitbag lashed across the thwarts at the front of the sledge, and I nodded.

"I'm ready," I said.

"What about your pistol?" Umeerinneq asked. "For bears."

"A pistol is no good," Tuukula said. He pointed at a long, soft leather case tied to one of the uprights at the back of the sledge. "I have a rifle."

"And my pistol is somewhere inside all these layers," I said, curious that I couldn't feel it, let alone find it. I hoped I wouldn't need it.

Tuukula clapped Umeerinneq on the shoulder, and said, "We'll be back before Wednesday. Don't worry. I'll look after your constable."

I almost laughed, settled for a smile, and then followed Tuukula back to the sledge, skirting wide around Cargo as the big dog glared at me. Tuukula pointed at a spot on the sledge behind Luui, then tugged a band of bone with two slits carved through the centre of it. He pushed the bone into Luui's hands, then helped her tie the sealskin cord around the back of her head.

"Sunglasses," he said. "From the old days."

The sun circled low in the sky, and the reflection on the ice was far softer than the middle of the day. I had the impression the Greenlandic sunglasses at this hour served another purpose, much like the aviator glasses Tuukula wore in the car. Tuukula confirmed it as he pulled out another pair, grinning as he fixed them in place, before quietly releasing the quick release anchor frozen into the ice.

The dogs twitched as Tuukula climbed onto the sledge. He hushed them with a growl, fidgeting behind me as he tugged the dog whip out from beneath a cord of sealskin.

"Ready," he whispered to Luui.

"Ready steady," she whispered back. Luui raised her hand, pressing a small thumb into the air.

"Hold onto my daughter," Tuukula said, as Luui let her hand drop.

"*Go*," she shouted, and the sledge leaped across the ice as the dogs leaned into the traces, clawing behind Spirit as she steered the team north to Siorapaluk.

Part 17

I held on to Luui, but the bumping and grating of the sledge, together with her wriggling back and forth over the kitbag, made me feel like I was trying to catch a basketball rolling across the deck of a boat in wild seas. Tuukula laughed, and I gave up, slipping my hands inside the pouch pocket at the front of my smock, letting the wind tug at my hair. Tuukula reached forwards, pulling the tip of my hood back to reveal my face. The hood fell flat against my neck and the wind flowed through my hair. I pulled the elastic from my ponytail, closed my eyes and revelled in the fresh Arctic breeze, the soft rays of the sun, and the gentle shush and grate of the sledge as the ice smoothed and the dogs found their rhythm. I felt invigorated and empowered by the land, willing to give up some city comforts – just for a little while – as we sank into the wild.

When I opened my eyes again, I found Luui crouched in front of me, staring into my face. She wriggled forwards, cupped her palms on my cheeks and traced my nose, my ears, and my eyes with the tips of her warm fingers. I wrinkled my nose as it tickled, and, when Luui giggled, I wrapped my arm around her, pulled her into my lap, and held on, just as Tuukula had asked me to.

We sledged through the night, as the sun swung behind the mountains, and the light faded just a little. Luui snored in my lap and I dozed in between, lifting my head each time Tuukula asked if I was warm, if I was hungry, if I was content?

Content.

I suppose I was. Out there on the ice, sledging north. But the very idea was so far removed from what I thought I would be doing in my first year as a police constable, it made me wonder. The commissioner would be accused of favouritism and Sergeant Jowls would do his best to derail and sabotage my new-found responsibilities. But in that moment, on Tuukula's sledge, with Luui snoring in my arms, even when she farted into her travelling furs, I realised I could cope with a little favouritism, if that's what it was.

I slept, hunched over Luui, until the dawn light and a slow sledge woke me. Luui was perched at the front of the sledge, watching her father, as Tuukula tickled the dog whip on the ice in front of the team, guiding the way around what looked to be bad ice. Water oozed through holes and cracks, spilling onto the surface, cooling from sea black to frost white as it spread.

"Hey," Tuukula said, as one of the wheel dogs closest to the runners drifted out to the right. "Hey. Hey." He growled when the dog didn't listen, then flicked the whip over the team, striking the ice to one side of the dog. The dog bumped into its neighbour, then yelped as Cargo nipped its flank, bringing the younger dog back into line, before jogging back to the number two position. Tuukula led the team in this way across two bays, before finally stopping the team on a patch of thick ice just off the shore.

"We're close," he said, as he pulled a small primus, pans and matches out of the sledge bag stretched between the two uprights.

I stared into the north, searching for the hut as Tuukula melted snow to make tea. He pressed an enamel mug into my hands, and a strip of dried whale meat into my mouth. Luui chewed at a long strip of meat, tilting her head and tugging at it like a Danish child might chew a strip of candy.

"Do you see it?" Tuukula asked as he sipped his tea.

"Not yet," I said.

I worked my teeth around the whale meat until I could chew. The tea helped.

"There." Tuukula pointed at a flat strip of black just above a white knoll of snow covering a boulder on the land. "That's the roof," he said.

"I see it."

There wasn't much to see, and I was impressed that he knew where to look. But another question nagged at me, and I chewed faster in order to ask it.

"You said Isaja disappeared that night."

"*Aap.*"

"But what you really mean, is that he sledged here, to this cabin."

"*Imaqa,*" Tuukula said. "He could have."

"That's quite a feat for a seven-year-old boy," I said.

"Powerful magic." Tuukula dipped his head to smile at Luui. "It runs in the family. It's in their blood."

I didn't doubt it. Nor did I doubt my gut instinct that the answers to Isaja's disappearance could be found in or around the old hut, just a few minutes away by dog sledge. I finished my tea, took another strip of whale meat, and chewed the rest of the way to the hut.

Part 18

Tuukula cut two loops in the ice to anchor the team, settling them with cubes of seal blubber. He stood over them, growling each time one dog tried to steal another dog's fat. I watched, fascinated, as the fat gooped from the dog's incisors and jaws as they chewed, gulped and swallowed. Tuukula waited until each dog was finished, and then walked back to the sledge to pick up the rifle. He slung it over his shoulder and nodded for Luui to walk on ahead.

"The hut is old," he said, as we clambered over the ice foot dividing the land from the frozen sea. "But useful in emergencies."

"But you wouldn't stay there for long?"

"Not unless I had to," Tuukula said. He paused as Luui said something, then beckoned for her to come quickly, stooping to pick her up as he slipped the rifle off his shoulder. Tuukula held Luui in one arm and clasped the rifle in the other, the stock against his hip.

"What is it?" I said, pulling back my hood and tilting my head, almost certain I had heard something on the wind. "Is it a bear?"

The sound of huffing, scraping, and snorting lilted over the snow-covered boulder, pricking Tuukula's senses, and causing Luui to curl her arms around his neck. I tugged at the V of my smock, lifting it before thrusting my hand inside the polar bear skin trousers, worming my fingers to my hip where I found the snap of the holster. I curled my fingers around the pistol grip and pulled it out of my trousers.

The standard issue 9mm Heckler and Koch USP Compact pistol held thirteen rounds. Too small to kill a bear, but I figured I had thirteen chances to scare it away. Long enough to give Tuukula a chance to kill it if need be. I felt my heart leap with skittish beats. I took several breaths, reining in my adrenaline a little, just enough for me to nod at Tuukula and point to the right of the boulder.

"I'll go that way," I said.

"I'll come with you."

I led the way, scuffing the soles of my sealskin *kamikker* over icy boulders, before breaking the crust of wind-leached snow. Tuukula nodded for me to keep going each time I turned to see where he was. The huffing and snorting grew louder, together with another sound, like rocks rolling and crashing to one side.

I reached the boulder and crouched in the snow beside it. The pistol cooled in my grasp and I wondered if I should wear gloves. But the thought vanished at the sound of a hoarse shout and the crack of a bullet zipping through the air towards us. Tuukula dropped onto his belly, flattening Luui in the snow beneath him as he lifted his head. He pointed to one side and I moved to my right as Tuukula slid the rifle into his shoulder, sighting up the rise, ready to fire if the bear were to suddenly lurch around the boulder. I paused at another shout, flinching at a second crack of a rifle.

"I'm going to take a look," I said, ignoring Tuukula as he started to protest.

With my pistol in one hand, I squirmed onto my belly and crawled the last few metres of the rise until I could see over the top. My breath caught in my throat as I saw a gaunt man with a long wispy beard and wavy black hair, naked but for a pair of threadbare *kamikker* on his feet, fiddling with the bolt of the rifle in his hands. I scanned left, away from the man standing in front of the dilapidated hut, then swore at the sight of a polar bear, poised above an exposed shallow grave of rocks, huffing from side to side as the man fired for a third time.

The third shot clapped into the snow in front of the grave, far short of the bear. The bear's creamy, matted flanks showed no signs of it being hit by the first two shots. It roared, rocking back onto its hind legs as I gripped my pistol in two hands, aimed above the bear's head, and fired three shots in quick succession. The bear lurched to one side and I fired another three shots, followed by two more, encouraging the bear as it dropped onto all fours and loped away to one side, before curling back across the land and racing towards the frozen sea.

"Firing," Tuukula said, as walked up beside me, chambered a round in his rifle and shot after the bear. I saw the puff of snow at the bear's heels as the crack of the rifle bullet echoed deeper than my own.

Tuukula lowered his rifle, flicked the safety switch and slung it over his shoulder as Luui clambered up the rise to take his hand. The three of us turned to look at the naked man shivering outside the hut. Tuukula squinted into the light, raised his hand to shield his eyes, before calling out to the man.

"Rassi?"

Part 19

It took me a moment to realise I was looking at a dead man, someone who had been missing for nearly three months. But more than that, the ghostlike appearance of the naked man standing in the snow outside the broken winds of the Arctic hut, was all the more haunting because of the way he stood, rocking his weight from foot to foot, not unlike the polar bear. This man was perhaps Rassi Qisuk, but whatever connection he once had to the village of Qaanaaq, to the people and his family who lived there was gone, replaced with the husk of a body barely supporting a feral mind. Tuukula called out his name one more time, and Rassi scurried back inside the hut.

"Tuukula," I said, placing my hand on his arm as he took a step forward.

"What?"

"Be careful."

"It's Rassi."

"He was once, maybe," I said, lowering my voice. "Not anymore."

Tuukula nodded, then spoke to Luui in Greenlandic, pressing her behind his body, and, I imagined, giving her strict instructions to walk behind him, and to stay there. I walked beside them, then nodded at the spot where the polar bear had been digging. I saw Rassi's pale face at the broken window, as I led Tuukula and Luui to the pile of rocks and small rounded boulders, coated in crisp black Arctic lichen.

The polar bear had removed the first layer of rocks. I slipped my pistol inside the pouch of my smock, and then held up my hand for Tuukula to stop, shaking my head at Luui as she peered around his legs, her fingers teasing at the fur of Tuukula's trousers. I knelt by the rock pile that I could now see was a grave, removing a couple more rocks, placing them gently to one side as I revealed the grey face of a small boy. His skin, dry, like parched leather, clung to his cheekbones. The boy's teeth were small and white beneath his curled lips. The shock of black hair on his head, so thick, startled my brain into thinking that his death was recent.

"Isaja," Tuukula whispered.

I looked up as the door of the hut creaked open. Rassi stepped out, tugging a length of twine through the waist loops of his jeans and tying it over his hip as he walked towards us. He buttoned his shirt as he drew close, stopping beside Tuukula before looking at me and at the boy in the grave at my feet.

"Rassi," I said. "My name is Constable Jensen. I've been looking for Isaja."

"My boy," Rassi said, the words rasping across his tongue.

"Yes," I said. "Is this Isaja?"

Rassi nodded, once, definitive.

"What happened, Rassi?"

I stood to one side as Rassi approached the grave. I noticed his quick-bitten nails at the ends of thin fingers, and the bony cut of his shoulders protruding from his shirt as he bent down to replace the rocks. I helped him as soon as Isaja's face was covered. Then, with Luui by my side and Tuukula next to Rassi, we replaced the last of the rocks disturbed by the bear. Rassi stood up, let his hands fall limp to his sides, and then turned to walk back to the hut.

"Go," Tuukula said. "Talk to him. Luui and I will fetch food from the sledge."

"Okay," I said, as I turned to follow Rassi.

The hut was surprisingly clean, with fine snow on the windowsills instead of dust. Sheets of newspaper lined the walls, peeling at the corners. Rassi sat down on the sleeping platform. We both stared at his rifle propped against the single chair beside the table. I took the rifle and placed it outside the hut. Rassi didn't move.

I pulled the chair out from the table and sat down, curious as to how to begin. Rassi saved me the trouble, clearing his voice with a cough before he started to speak. I reached inside my smock and tugged my notebook from my shirt pocket to record his story.

"Isaja ran away," he said, in a halting but clear Danish. "A long time ago. I was angry, too angry to look for him. I thought he would come back. Maybe he had been with his *ata*. Maybe he was with Tuukula. I even thought he could be with his *anaana* in Ilulissat. The social workers could have sent him there, paid for the ticket." He looked up with lifeless eyes. "But they didn't."

"No," I said, softly. I rested my notebook in my

lap and Rassi continued.

"It took a long time for me to realise that he wasn't coming back, that it might even be my fault. I was so angry. So angry I told everybody that Aluusaq had killed my son. That he did it to spite me. But no one believed me. Then, when I stopped drinking, I heard someone talk about missing dogs. Another man said someone had stolen his sledge. No one steals sledges, maybe they borrow dogs. But what I heard made me think, and then I knew that Isaja had gone somewhere."

"You thought he came here?"

"Not at first. This was an accident. First, I went deeper into the fjord, to Qeqertat. But Isaja was not there. Then I crossed the fjord to Herbert Island. He wasn't there either. I didn't want to go to Savissivik, in the south. But I told myself I would if I didn't find him in Siorapaluk. So I sledged north," Rassi said, pausing as Tuukula and Luui entered the hut. Rassi nodded when Tuukula offered him tea. The primus spat and the ice popped and cracked as it melted in the pan. Rassi continued. "I found tracks leading up to the hut, and I followed them, but then the sledge broke through thin ice. I was so excited about the tracks; I didn't think about the ice. When the sledge started to sink, I had to cut the dogs' traces. They ran, free of the sledge, leaving me alone on the ice." Rassi looked up at Tuukula, and said, "There was nothing I could do."

"And the dogs ran to Siorapaluk," I said. "The people there thought you were dead."

"When a team arrives without a sledge, it's easy to think the driver is dead."

"But you didn't die, Rassi," Tuukula said. He poured the tea, gave Rassi a mug, adding plenty of sugar, before settling on the floor with Luui in his lap.

"I wish I had," Rassi said. "Because when I came to the hut…"

I waited for Rassi to say more, encouraging him when he didn't. "You found your son inside the hut."

Rassi nodded, pressing his palm to his bony cheek to stem the flood of tears.

"He was dead when you found him," I said. "Wasn't he?"

"He lay here," Rassi said, patting the sleeping platform. "He lay very still. He had his arms wrapped around that bloody tooth. I buried him with it, lay the tooth on top of his grave. But it is gone now. I went out hunting one day, found tracks by Isaja's grave, and the tooth was gone." Rassi swallowed, took a sip of tea, and then looked up. "Isaja must have starved to death. It was my fault."

Rassi dipped his head to his knees. The tea slopped over the lip of his mug as he sobbed. I turned at a soft scratching sound, and watched as Luui crawled off her father's lap, padded across the floor, and slipped her hands around Rassi's arm. Luui wormed her way to Rassi's chest, and I watched, brushing at my own tears trickling down my cheeks, as the tiny girl comforted her half-brother's father.

"Rassi," I said, after a few minutes of silence. "We're going to take you and Isaja home."

Part 20

I helped Tuukula wrap Isaja's body in a tarpaulin. We carried him to a small sledge propped against the side of the hut, securing him for the journey back to Qaanaaq before pushing the sledge down to the ice. I watched as Tuukula ran a line from Isaja's sledge to his own.

"There must have been dogs. The dogs that brought Isaja and the tooth here," I said, as Tuukula finished tying his knots. "Why didn't Rassi use them to sledge back to Qaanaaq?"

"He let them go," Tuukula said.

"Why?"

"He never wanted to leave."

"But he's coming with us now. What's changed?"

Tuukula nodded at the shore where Luui helped Rassi over the ice foot.

"I told you powerful magic runs in this family. She's convinced him to come home."

I waited for Tuukula to smile, or to laugh, only to realise he was deadly serious.

"Umeerinneq told me you're a shaman. Luui said you were *angakkoq*."

"Maybe I am."

"But aren't shaman supposed to make *Tupilaq* and swim down to comb Sedna's hair?"

"So the stories say." Tuukula shrugged. "There's all kinds of magic in this world, Constable. I like to think everybody can use it."

"Like Isaja disappearing?"

"*Aap.* Exactly like that. I think, Constable," he said, "you are also a shaman."

"I doubt that," I said, with a laugh.

"You don't think so? How else did you find the boy?"

"Police work isn't magic, Tuukula."

"No? Then tell me how you found a boy who's been missing for nearly a year, when everyone else failed?"

"I asked the right people the right questions," I said. "That's all."

"*Naamik,*" Tuukula said. "That's magic."

The light caught his eye as he smiled and I decided I would let him have his way, agreeing that there *might* be some magic in this world after all.

We sledged back to Qaanaaq, towing Isaja's body behind Tuukula's sledge. Rassi and Tuukula took turns to rest and drive the team. Rassi seemed to grow stronger each time he gripped the dog whip, his commands clearer and more precise with every kilometre we sledged. Luui curled up in her father's arms, pinching his nose between her finger and thumb, giggling each time he pretended to bite her. I sat quietly, content to take in the sight of the brown mountain rock, the glaciers tonguing the valleys, the pant of the dogs and the fresh tang of salt, sea and ice. I knew I would miss it, but as I slept on the sledge, I confess to thinking about a hot shower, the soft mattress of my bed, and Sunday brunch at *Katuaq*. My first missing persons case had taken me to the top of Greenland, and I had drunk deeply of the raw, wild nature and the strange magic there. But after a week, I was ready to return to the city.

I spent my last few days in Qaanaaq accompanying Umeerinneq, sleeping in the guest bedroom of the police house, and wandering the gravel streets in the late light each evening. My walks always ended by the row of small hunters' cabins looking out onto the sea, where Tuukula sat and smoked, where there was always fresh spiced tea and a hint of magic in the air.

"I'm going to miss this," I said, watching Luui chase her friends around the drying racks, as Tuukula smoked his single cigarette.

"You'll be back, one day," he said.

"Yes, I know. But I mean *this*, Tuukula. The time I spent with you and Luui."

"It sounds like you think this is the last time we'll see each other."

"Isn't it? Nuuk is a long way away, and I'll be stuck in the city most of the time."

"Stuck in the city," Tuukula said. He laughed as he finished his cigarette. "You've changed."

"No," I said. "I don't think so."

"We'll see," he said, standing up. "*And* we'll see each other again."

"Where are you going?"

"I promised Rassi that I would sit with him when he visited his father. They have a lot to talk about. I said I would help. Do you want to come?"

"In a minute," I said.

I waved at Luui, catching her eye, and beckoning her over. The dust plumed from her heels as she picked up speed, skidding to a stop as she bumped into my knees.

"Happy Birthday, Luui," I said, pressing a tube of toothpaste into her hands. Luui beamed, opening the cap as she twirled away. "Erm, that wasn't quite what I had in mind," I said, as I watched her squeeze a gob of paste onto each of her friends' fingers. Tuukula laughed as the kids thrust their fingers into their mouths, licking at the frothy paste as it bubbled over their lips.

Part 21

The day after I arrived back in Nuuk, I noticed something odd about the surface of my desk beneath the staircase. Where there was once a single dusty box of papers there were now three. The telephone unit had been replaced with something more modern, and a call waiting light flashed red under one of the buttons.

"Don't get any grand ideas," Sergeant Duneq said, as he approached my desk. "This is a temporary assignment. You'll be back on the street and back on nights as soon as I convince the commissioner that you've still got a lot to learn. You're not…"

"Training anymore," I said, finishing the sergeant's sentence.

"What's that, Constable? Are you mocking me?"

"No, Sergeant. Not at all."

"Good." Duneq glanced at the light flashing on the phone and nodded at it. "You've got a call, Constable. I suggest you answer it."

"Yes, Sergeant."

I waited for Duneq to turn his back before I allowed myself a discreet but smug smile. Things were looking up, and the new phone, clean desk, and old files suggested that the commissioner intended to keep me busy.

"At least for a little while," I said, softly, as Duneq left the room.

I took a breath, pulled out the chair, and reached for the phone.

"Greenland Missing Persons desk," I said, as I sat down.

The chair tipped forwards, crashing into the floor as the two remaining wheels rolled backwards. If I hadn't been preoccupied breaking my fall, I might have heard the sergeant's deep guffaw from just outside the door.

Training might be over, but some things were just beginning.

The End

Author's Note

So now you've met Tuukula and his daughter Luui. I hope you like them, because you'll meet them again – often. In the introduction, I said there was no *grand plan*, but that was perhaps a half-truth, and I hope you'll forgive me. I have *big* plans for this series of novellas, with at least twenty stories planned in my head. In my later stories, set in the far future, Petra is a police commissioner, and I am excited to explore just how she got there. *The Boy with the Narwhal Tooth* is the most recent step, but not the first.

Petra was investigating *missing persons* in my first Maratse novel: *Seven Graves, One Winter*, published on Valentine's Day in 2018. But she actually appears for the very first time in a novella called *Container*, published on December 6, 2017. So, it's not such a stretch to explore how it all began.

Will there be inconsistencies in these stories? Will Petra actually have seen and experienced more of Greenland and its culture than she lets on when meeting and falling in love with Maratse?

Sure.

But hey, everyone's got secrets.

I hope you enjoyed *The Boy with the Narwhal Tooth*. I certainly enjoyed writing it.

Chris
June 2020
Denmark

About the Author

Christoffer Petersen is the author's pen name. He lives in Denmark. Chris started writing stories about Greenland while teaching in Qaanaaq, the largest village in the very north of Greenland – the population peaked at 600 during the two years he lived there. Chris spent a total of seven years in Greenland, teaching in remote communities and at the Police Academy in the capital of Nuuk.

Chris continues to be inspired by the vast icy wilderness of the Arctic and his books have a common setting in the region, with a Scandinavian influence. He has also watched enough Bourne movies to no longer be surprised by the plot, but not enough to get bored.

You can find Chris in Denmark or online here:

www.christoffer-petersen.com

By the Same Author

THE GREENLAND CRIME SERIES
featuring Constable David Maratse
SEVEN GRAVES, ONE WINTER Book 1
BLOOD FLOE Book 2
WE SHALL BE MONSTERS Book 3
INSIDE THE BEAR'S CAGE Book 4
WHALE HEART Book 5

Short Stories from the same series

KATABATIC
CONTAINER
TUPILAQ
THE LAST FLIGHT
THE HEART THAT WAS A WILD GARDEN
QIVITTOQ
THE THUNDER SPIRITS
ILULIAQ
SCRIMSHAW
ASIAQ
CAMP CENTURY
INUK
DARK CHRISTMAS
POISON BERRY
NORTHERN MAIL
SIKU

VIRUSI
THE WOMEN'S KNIFE
ICE, WIND & FIRE

THE GREENLAND TRILOGY
featuring Konstabel Fenna Brongaard
THE ICE STAR Book 1
IN THE SHADOW OF THE MOUNTAIN Book 2
THE SHAMAN'S HOUSE Book 3

MADE IN DENMARK
Short Stories featuring Milla Moth set in Denmark
DANISH DESIGN Story 1

THE POLARPOL ACTION THRILLERS
featuring Sergeant Petra "Piitalaat" Jensen,
Etienne Gagnon, Hákon Sigurðsson & more
NORTHERN LIGHT Book 1
MOUNTAIN GHOST Book 2

THE DETECTIVE FREJA HANSEN SERIES
set in Denmark and Scotland
FELL RUNNER Introductory novella
BLACKOUT INGÉNUE

THE WOLF CRIMES SERIES
set in Denmark, Alaska and Ukraine
PAINT THE DEVIL Book 1
LOST IN THE WOODS Book 2
CHERNOBYL WOLVES Book 3

THE WHEELMAN SHORTS
Short Stories featuring Noah Lee set in Australia

PULP DRIVER Story 1

THE DARK ADVENT SERIES
*featuring Police Commissioner
Petra "Piitalaat" Jensen set in Greenland*
THE CALENDAR MAN Book 1
THE TWELFTH NIGHT Book 2
INVISIBLE TOUCH Book 3
NORTH STAR BAY Book 4

UNDERCOVER GREENLAND
featuring Eko Simigaq and Inniki Rasmussen
NARKOTIKA Book 1

CAPTAIN ERRONEOUS SMITH
featuring Captain Erroneous Smith
THE ICE CIRCUS Book 1

THE BOLIVIAN GIRL
a hard-hitting military and political thriller series
THE BOLIVIAN GIRL Book 1

GUERRILLA GREENLAND
featuring Constable David Maratse
ARCTIC STATE Novella 1
ARCTIC REBEL Novella 2
GREENLAND MISSING PERSONS novellas
featuring Constable Petra "Piitalaat" Jensen
THE BOY WITH THE NARWHAL TOOTH
THE GIRL WITH THE RAVEN TONGUE
THE SHIVER IN THE ARCTIC
THE FEVER IN THE WATER